·THE· PATCHWORK QUILT

by VALERIE FLOURNOY
pictures by JERRY PINKNEY

Dial Books for Young Readers
New York

Published by
Dial Books for Young Readers
A Division of NAL Penguin Inc.
2 Park Avenue
New York, New York 10016

Design by Susan Lu
Printed in Hong Kong by South China Printing Co.
W
10   9   8

Library of Congress Cataloging in Publication Data
Flournoy, Valerie, 1952– The patchwork quilt.
Summary: Using scraps cut from the family's old clothing,
Tanya helps her grandmother make a beautiful quilt
that tells the story of her family's life.
[Quilting—Fiction. 2. Grandmothers—Fiction.
3. Family life—Fiction.   4. Afro-Americans—Fiction.]
I. Pinkney, Jerry, ill.   II. Title.
PZ7.F667Pat 1984   [E]   84-1711
ISBN 0-8037-0097-0
ISBN 0-8037-0098-9 (lib. bdg.)

The art for each picture consists of a pencil, graphite,
and watercolor painting, which is camera-separated
and reproduced in full color.

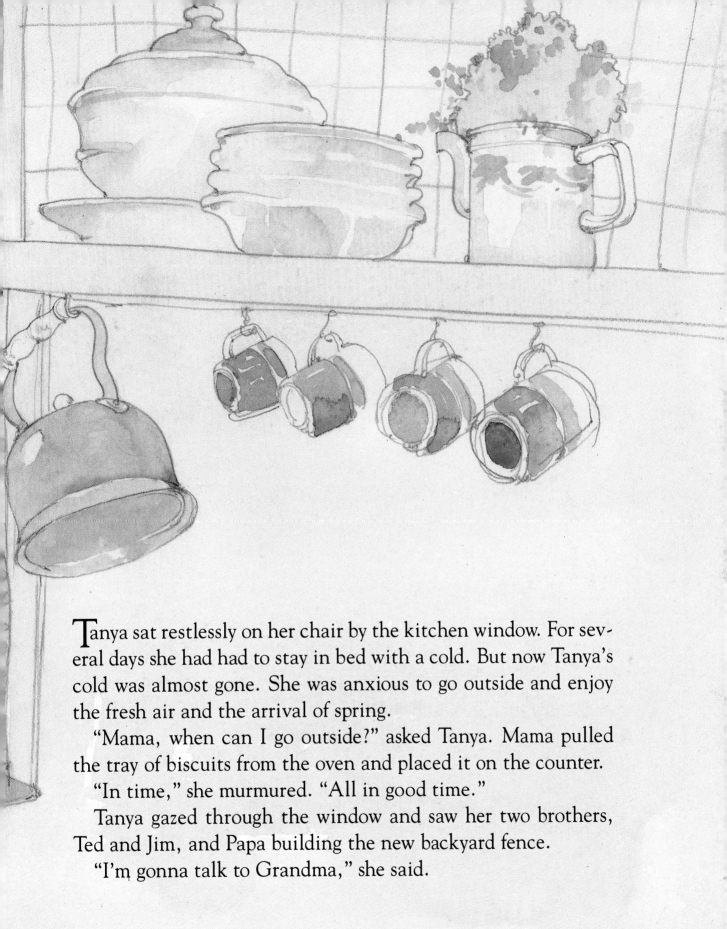

Tanya sat restlessly on her chair by the kitchen window. For several days she had had to stay in bed with a cold. But now Tanya's cold was almost gone. She was anxious to go outside and enjoy the fresh air and the arrival of spring.

"Mama, when can I go outside?" asked Tanya. Mama pulled the tray of biscuits from the oven and placed it on the counter.

"In time," she murmured. "All in good time."

Tanya gazed through the window and saw her two brothers, Ted and Jim, and Papa building the new backyard fence.

"I'm gonna talk to Grandma," she said.

Grandma was sitting in her favorite spot—the big soft chair in front of the picture window. In her lap were scraps of materials of all textures and colors. Tanya recognized some of them. The plaid was from Papa's old work shirt, and the red scraps were from the shirt Ted had torn that winter.

"Whatcha gonna do with all that stuff?" Tanya asked.

"Stuff? These ain't stuff. These little pieces gonna make me a quilt, a patchwork quilt."

Tanya tilted her head. "I know what a quilt is, Grandma. There's one on your bed, but it's old and dirty and Mama can never get it clean."

Grandma sighed. "It ain't dirty, honey. It's worn, the way it's supposed to be."

Grandma flexed her fingers to keep them from stiffening. She sucked in some air and said, "My mother made me a quilt when I wasn't any older than you. But sometimes the old ways are forgotten."

Tanya leaned against the chair and rested her head on her grandmother's shoulder.

Just then Mama walked in with two glasses of milk and some biscuits. Mama looked at the scraps of material that were scattered all over. "Grandma," she said, "I just cleaned this room, and now it's a mess."

"It's not a mess, Mama," Tanya said through a mouthful of biscuit. "It's a quilt."

"A quilt! You don't need these scraps. I can get you a quilt," Mama said.

Grandma looked at her daughter and then turned to her grandchild. "Yes, your mama can get you a quilt from any department store. But it won't be like my patchwork quilt, and it won't last as long either."

Mama looked at Grandma, then picked up Tanya's empty glass and went to make lunch.

Grandma's eyes grew dark and distant. She turned away from Tanya and gazed out the window, absentmindedly rubbing the pieces of material through her fingers.

"Grandma, I'll help you make your quilt," Tanya said.

"Thank you, honey."

"Let's start right now. We'll be finished in no time."

Grandma held Tanya close and patted her head. "It's gonna take quite a while to make this quilt, not a couple of days or a week—not even a month. A good quilt, a masterpiece..." Grandma's eyes shone at the thought. "Why I need more material. More gold and blue, some red and green. And I'll need the time to do it right. It'll take me a year at least."

"A year," shouted Tanya. "That's too long. I can't wait that long, Grandma."

Grandma laughed. "A year ain't that long, honey. Makin' this quilt gonna be a joy. Now run along and let Grandma rest." Grandma turned her head toward the sunlight and closed her eyes.

"I'm gonna make a masterpiece," she murmured, clutching a scrap of cloth in her hand, just before she fell asleep.

"We'll have to get you a new pair and use these old ones for rags," Mama said as she hung the last piece of wash on the clothesline one August afternoon.

Jim was miserable. His favorite blue corduroy pants had been held together with patches; now they were beyond repair.

"Bring them here," Grandma said.

Grandma took part of the pant leg and cut a few blue squares. Jim gave her a hug and watched her add his patches to the others.

"A quilt won't forget. It can tell your life story," she said.

The arrival of autumn meant school and Halloween. This year Tanya would be an African princess. She danced around in the long, flowing robes Mama had made from several yards of colorful material. The old bracelets and earrings Tanya had found in a trunk in the attic jingled noisily as she moved. Grandma cut some squares out of the leftover scraps and added Tanya to the quilt too!

The days grew colder but Tanya and her brothers didn't mind. They knew snow wasn't far away. Mama dreaded winter's coming. Every year she would plead with Grandma to move away from the drafty window, but Grandma wouldn't budge.

"Grandma, please," Mama scolded. "You can sit here by the heater."

"I'm not your grandmother, I'm your mother," Grandma said. "And I'm gonna sit here in the Lord's light and make my masterpiece."

It was the end of November when Ted, Jim, and Tanya got their wish. They awoke one morning to find everything in sight covered with snow. Tanya got dressed and flew down the stairs. Ted and Jim, and even Mama and Papa, were already outside.

"I don't like leaving Grandma in that house by herself," Mama said. "I know she's lonely."

Tanya pulled herself out of the snow being careful not to ruin her angel. "Grandma isn't lonely," Tanya said happily. "She and the quilt are telling each other stories."

Mama glanced questioningly at Tanya, "Telling each other stories?"

"Yes, Grandma says a quilt never forgets!"

The family spent the morning and most of the afternoon sledding down the hill. Finally, when they were all numb from the cold, they went inside for hot chocolate and sandwiches.

"I think I'll go sit and talk to Grandma," Mama said.

"Then she can explain to you about our quilt—our very own family quilt," Tanya said.

Mama saw the mischievous glint in her youngest child's eyes.

"Why, I may just have her do that, young lady," Mama said as she walked out of the kitchen.

Tanya leaned over the table to see into the living room. Grandma was hunched over, her eyes close to the fabric as she made tiny stitches. Mama sat at the old woman's feet. Tanya couldn't hear what was said but she knew Grandma was telling Mama all about quilts and how *this* quilt would be very special. Tanya sipped her chocolate slowly, then she saw Mama pick up a piece of fabric, rub it with her fingers, and smile.

From that moment on both women spent their winter evenings working on the quilt. Mama did the sewing while Grandma cut the fabrics and placed the scraps in a pattern of colors. Even while they were cooking and baking all their Christmas specialties during the day, at night they still worked on the quilt. Only once did Mama put it aside. She wanted to wear something special Christmas night, so she bought some gold material and made a beautiful dress. Tanya knew without asking that the gold scraps would be in the quilt too.

There was much singing and laughing that Christmas. All Grandma's sons and daughters and nieces and nephews came to pay their respects. The Christmas tree lights shone brightly, filling the room with sparkling colors. Later, when everyone had gone home, Papa said he had never felt so much happiness in the house. And Mama agreed.

When Tanya got downstairs the next morning, she found Papa fixing pancakes.

"Is today a special day too?" asked Jim.

"Where's Mama?" asked Tanya.

"Grandma doesn't feel well this morning," Papa said. "Your mother is with her now till the doctor gets here."

"Will Grandma be all right?" Ted asked.

Papa rubbed his son's head and smiled. "There's nothing for you to worry about. We'll take care of Grandma."

Tanya looked into the living room. There on the back of the big chair rested the patchwork quilt. It was folded neatly, just as Grandma had left it.

"Mother didn't want us to know she wasn't feeling well. She thought it would spoil our Christmas," Mama told them later, her face drawn and tired, her eyes a puffy red. "Now it's up to all of us to be quiet and make her as comfortable as possible." Papa put an arm around Mama's shoulder.

"Can we see Grandma?" Tanya asked.

"No, not tonight," Papa said. "Grandma needs plenty of rest."

It was nearly a week, the day before New Year's, before the children were permitted to see their grandmother. She looked tired and spoke in whispers.

"We miss you, Grandma," Ted said.

"And your muffins and hot chocolate," added Jim. Grandma smiled.

"Your quilt misses you too, Grandma," Tanya said. Grandma's smile faded from her lips. Her eyes grew cloudy.

"My masterpiece," Grandma sighed. "It would have been beautiful. Almost half finished." The old woman closed her eyes and turned away from her grandchildren. Papa whispered it was time to leave. Ted, Jim, and Tanya crept from the room.

Tanya walked slowly to where the quilt lay. She had seen Grandma and Mama work on it. Tanya thought real hard. She knew how to cut the scraps, but she wasn't certain of the rest. Just then Tanya felt a hand resting on her shoulder. She looked up and saw Mama.

"Tomorrow," Mama said.

New Year's Day was the beginning. After the dishes were washed and put away, Tanya and Mama examined the quilt.

"You cut more squares, Tanya, while I stitch some patches together," Mama said.

Tanya snipped and trimmed the scraps of material till her hands hurt from the scissors. Mama watched her carefully, making sure the squares were all the same size. The next day was the same as the last. More snipping and cutting. But Mama couldn't always be around to watch Tanya work. Grandma had to be looked after. So Tanya worked by herself. Then one night, as Papa read them stories, Jim walked over and looked at the quilt. In it he saw patches of blue. His blue. Without saying a word Jim picked up the scissors and some scraps and started to make squares. Ted helped Jim put the squares in piles while Mama showed Tanya how to join them.

Every day, as soon as she got home from school, Tanya worked on the quilt. Ted and Jim were too busy with sports, and Mama was looking after Grandma, so Tanya worked alone. But after a few weeks she stopped. Something was wrong—something was missing, Tanya thought. For days the quilt lay on the back of the chair. No one knew why Tanya had stopped working. Tanya would sit and look at the quilt. Finally she knew. Some*thing* wasn't missing. Some*one* was missing from the quilt.

That evening before she went to bed Tanya tiptoed into Grandma's room, a pair of scissors in her hand. She quietly lifted the end of Grandma's old quilt and carefully removed a few squares.

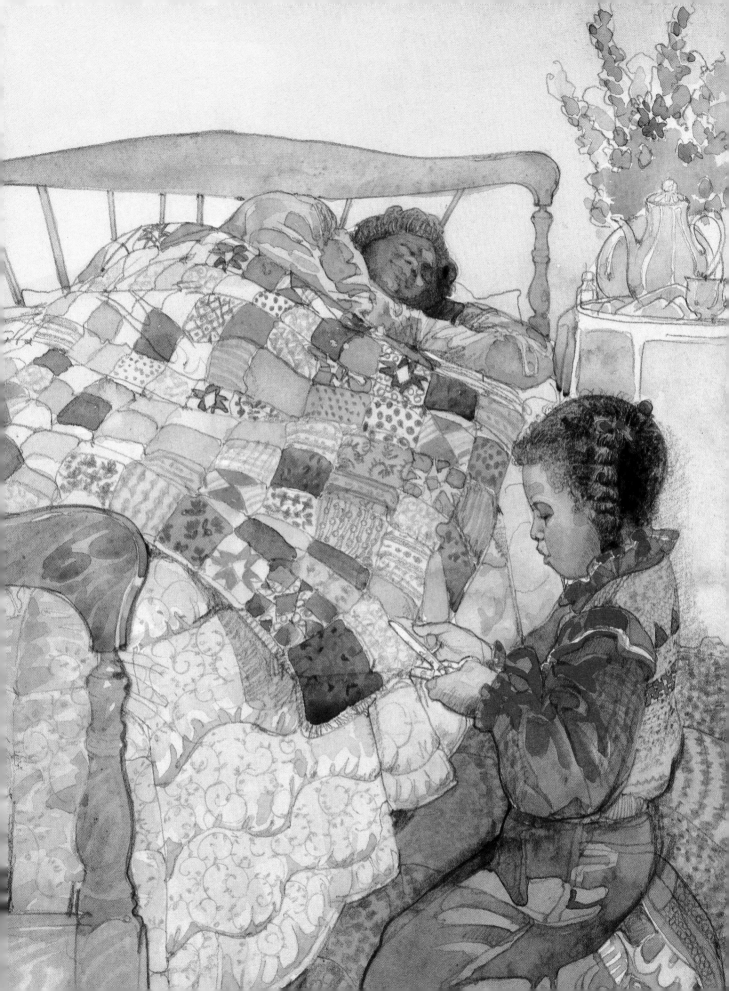

February and March came and went as Mama proudly watched her daughter work on the last few rows of patches. Tanya always found time for the quilt. Grandma had been watching too. The old woman had been getting stronger and stronger as the months passed. Once she was able, Papa would carry Grandma to her chair by the window. "I needs the Lord's light," Grandma said. Then she would sit and hum softly to herself and watch Tanya work.

"Yes, honey, this quilt is nothin' but a joy," Grandma said.

Summer vacation was almost here. One June day Tanya came home to find Grandma working on the quilt again! She had finished sewing the last few squares together; the stuffing was in place, and she was already pinning on the backing.

"Grandma!" Tanya shouted.

Grandma looked up. "Hush, child. It's almost time to do the quilting on these patches. But first I have some special finishing touches...."

The next night Grandma cut the final thread with her teeth. "There. It's done," she said. Mama helped Grandma spread the quilt full length.

Nobody had realized how big it had gotten or how beautiful. Reds, greens, blues, and golds, light shades and dark, blended in and out throughout the quilt.

"It's beautiful," Papa said. He touched the gold patch, looked at Mama, and remembered. Jim remembered too. There was his blue and the red from Ted's shirt. There was Tanya's Halloween costume. And there was Grandma. Even though her patch was old, it fit right in.

They all remembered the past year. They especially remembered Tanya and all her work. So it had been decided. In the right hand corner of the last row of patches was delicately stitched, "For Tanya from your Mama and Grandma."

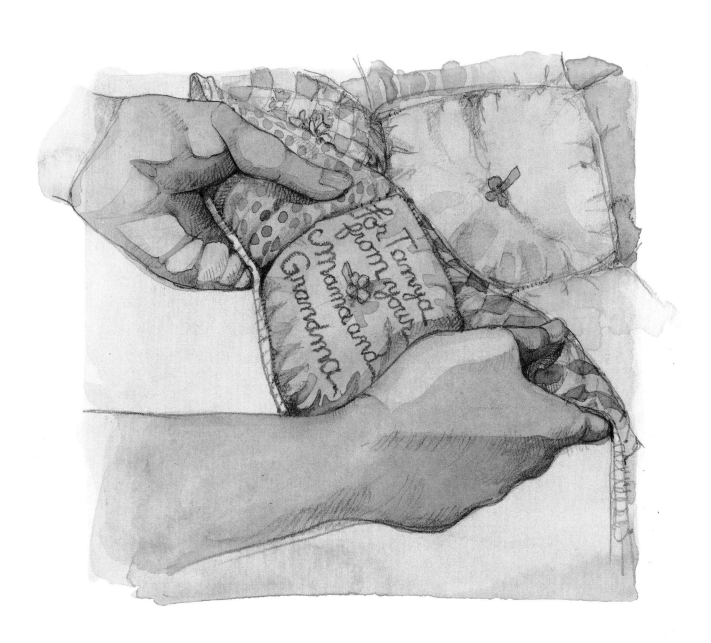